CYNTHIA RYLANT

POPPLETON
and Friends

BOOK TWO

Illustrated by
MARK TEAGUE

THE BLUE SKY PRESS
An Imprint of Scholastic Inc. · New York

For Thrity
C. R.

To John and Alex
M. T.

THE BLUE SKY PRESS

Text copyright © 1997 by Cynthia Rylant
Illustrations copyright © 1997 by Mark Teague

Library of Congress Cataloging-in-Publication Data
Rylant, Cynthia.
Poppleton and friends / Cynthia Rylant;
illustrated by Mark Teague.   p.   cm
Summary: Poppleton the pig goes to the beach, solves a lint
mystery, and learns that friends are the secret to a long life.
ISBN 0-590-84786-4
[1. Pigs — Fiction. 2. Friendship — Fiction.
3. Beaches — Fiction.] I. Teague, Mark, ill. II. Title.
PZ7.R9822Pr 1997 [E] — dc20 96-3366 CIP AC
12 11 10 9 8 7 6 5 4 3 2 1
Printed in the United States of America
First printing, September 1997   37
Production supervision by Angela Biola
Designed by Kathleen Westray

CONTENTS

THE SHORE DAY

Poppleton was tired of
being landlocked.
He wanted to go to the shore.

"Hudson likes the shore,"
said Poppleton.
"I'll ask him to go, too."

Soon Poppleton and Hudson were
on a bus, heading for the shore.

There were a lot of older ladies
on the bus.
They were a club.
They called themselves
"The Sassy Sues."

Hudson and Poppleton enjoyed

the ladies very much.

The ladies taught them new songs,

and new dances,

and how to win at poker.

When the bus got to the shore,
Hudson and Poppleton waved
good-bye to the ladies.

Poppleton had a big beach chair,
which he unfolded.
Hudson had a little beach chair,
which he unfolded.

They ate cheese sandwiches.

They watched the waves.

They collected shells.

At the end of the day,
they took the bus back home.
"Let's tell Cherry Sue about
our day," said Poppleton.

Hudson and Poppleton went to see
Cherry Sue.
They gave her some shells
and a cheese sandwich.

They sang her some new songs.
They danced her some new dances.
They taught her how to win
at poker.

They were very happy.

The shore day had been great.

But remembering it was even better.

DRY SKIN

Poppleton looked in the mirror
one morning.
"Yikes!" he cried. "Dry skin!"
He looked closer.
"I am flaking away."

Poppleton called Cherry Sue.

"Cherry Sue," said Poppleton,

"I am as dry as an old apple.

What should I do?"

"Put on some oil," said Cherry Sue.

"All right," said Poppleton.

He put on some oil.

But the next day, the dry skin was back.

Poppleton called Cherry Sue again.

"I am as dry as a dandelion,"

said Poppleton.

"Did you put on some oil?"

asked Cherry Sue.

"It didn't help," said Poppleton.

"It just made me want french fries."

"Then put on some honey,"
said Cherry Sue.
"All right," said Poppleton.
He put on some honey.

But the next day, the dry skin was back.

Poppleton called Cherry Sue.

"I am as dry as a desert," said Poppleton.

"Did you put on some honey?"

asked Cherry Sue.

"It didn't help," said Poppleton.

"It just made me want biscuits."

"I'll be right over," said Cherry Sue.

When she walked into Poppleton's house,
Cherry Sue saw twenty empty french fry
bags and a chair full of crumbs.
"Told you," said Poppleton.
"Let me see your dry skin,"
said Cherry Sue.
Poppleton leaned over.
Cherry Sue looked closely.

"Poppleton, you don't have dry skin!"
said Cherry Sue.

"I don't?" asked Poppleton.

"You have *lint*!" said Cherry Sue.

"Lint?" asked Poppleton.

"Where did I get lint?"

"From that old sweater,"
said Cherry Sue.

"Poppleton, have you been wearing
the same linty sweater for three days?"
asked Cherry Sue.

Poppleton hung his head.

"I can be such a pig," he said.

"I'll be right back," said Cherry Sue.
Soon she came back with a lint brush.
"No llama can be without one," she said.
Poppleton brushed away the lint,

and threw away the bags,
and swept away the crumbs.

"I feel like a new pig,"
Poppleton said to Cherry Sue.
"You look like one," said Cherry Sue.
"Especially with that new wart
on your nose."

"WART?!!!" Poppleton screamed,
running for the mirror.

Cherry Sue giggled all the way home.

GRAPEFRUIT

One day Poppleton was watching TV.
The man on TV said grapefruit made
people live longer.
Poppleton hated grapefruit.
But he wanted to live longer.
He wanted to live to be one hundred.

So he went to the store

and brought home some grapefruit.

He cut it up and took a little taste.
Poppleton's lips turned outside-in.

He took another little taste.

Poppleton's eyes made tears.

He took the tiniest taste
he could possibly take.

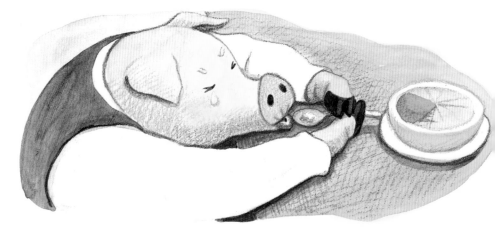

Poppleton's face turned green.

Poppleton's friend Hudson knocked
at the door.

"Poppleton, why are you all green?"
Hudson cried.

"And where are your lips?"

"I am eating grapefruit to live longer,"
said Poppleton. "And it
is making me sick."
"Then don't eat it!" cried Hudson.
"But I want to live to be one hundred,"
said Poppleton.
"With no lips?" asked Hudson.
"What else can I do?" asked Poppleton.
"Wait here," said Hudson.

Soon he was back with
a very, very, very old mouse.
"This is my Uncle Bill," said Hudson.
"Uncle Bill, tell Poppleton
how you lived to be one hundred."

Uncle Bill nodded.

He leaned over to Poppleton.

"Friends," he said.

"Friends?" asked Poppleton.

"Friends," said Uncle Bill. "What
did you do with your lips?"

When Uncle Bill and Hudson left,
Poppleton threw all of
the grapefruit away.
And as soon as his lips came back,

he went out to find some friends.